The Day the Snapdragons Snapped Back

by Melinda Chambers

illustrated by Sue Ann Spiker

Headline Kids
an imprint of Headline Books, Inc.
Terra Alta, WV

The Day the Snapdragons Snapped Back

by Melinda Chambers

illustrated by Sue Ann Spiker

To order additional copies of this book
or for book publishing information, or to contact the author:

Headline Kids
P.O. Box 52
Terra Alta, WV 26764
www.headlinebooks.com

Tel/Fax: 800-570-5951
Email: mybook@headlinebooks.com

www.headlinebooks.com
www.headlinekids.com
www.MelindaChambers.com

Headline Kids is an imprint of Headline Books

Colorful Springs Snapdragon©Rebekah Burgess United States

ISBN 0-929915-72-0
ISBN-13: 9780929915722

Library of Congress Control Number: 2007932789

PRINTED IN THE UNITED STATES OF AMERICA

Dedication

To your future.
May you cultivate
what life has in store
for you and bloom in
radiant colors.

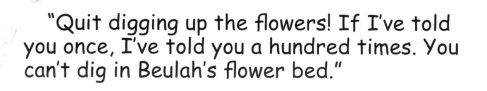

"Quit digging up the flowers! If I've told you once, I've told you a hundred times. You can't dig in Beulah's flower bed."

"But I buried a bone in here last week, and I want it."

"Miss Beulah will be quite upset with you when she sees what you've done to her beautiful flowers."

"Oh, Beulah's too nice to be mad for very long. Besides, I'm too cute to yell at...and they're JUST flowers. She won't miss a few."

"You young pups are all alike. You think you can just do anything you want and nothing bad will happen. But sometimes things happen that you don't expect—that you can't change. You need to be prepared. Come sit by me and I'll tell you a story."

Finding the lost
bone, and eager to
gnaw on it for awhile,
the pup snuggled up
to his mom and was
ALL EARS.

11

"Back before you were born—in fact, I wasn't very old myself—I watched as Beulah planted some snapdragons in her flower bed.

"Every morning she checked on them, watered them if they needed it, removed the weeds from around them, and gave them fertilizer to help them grow. With such good care, it wasn't long before they started to grow. But little did she know that disaster was looming just around the corner...

13

"One morning real early, just as the buds were beginning to spring into beautiful flowers, a couple of chipmunks came through and terrorized the flower bed.

"They grabbed those flowers and started to whittle them just above the surface of the ground, taking the buds with them.

"When Beulah came out to water her flowers later that morning, she couldn't believe what she saw.

"All that was left of her beautiful snapdragons was stems barely sticking out of the ground. Gone were the multi-colored blooms Beulah planned to enjoy all summer. Gone were the rewards from her hard work. Gone were her dreams.

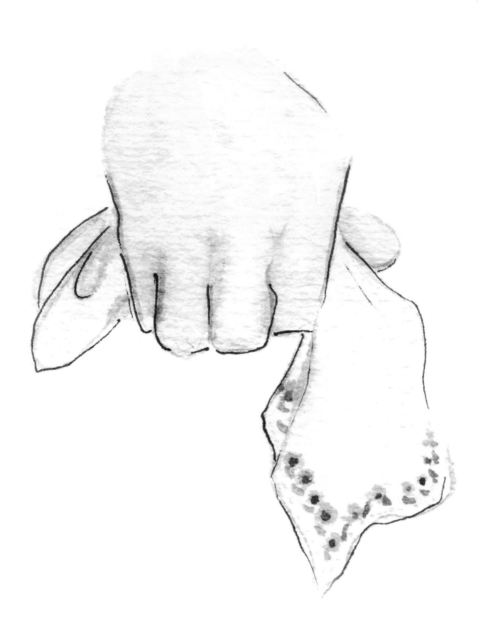

"Wiping away her tears, she went back inside, vowing never to plant snapdragons again."

"Poor Beulah. What happened then?" asked the puppy.

"Every morning I checked on those snapdragons, or what was LEFT of them. Little by little they started to grow back.

"With the help of the summer rains and the warm sun, the meager stems were transformed. In no time, it seemed, those snapdragons had SNAPPED BACK. In fact, there were snapdragons everywhere."

"How did they do that?"

"Well, even though the chipmunks took away the plant that showed on the surface, they didn't get to the roots. That was where the heart of the plant was. With help from nature, the plant was able to come back, this time even sturdier than it was before."

"What did Beulah do when she saw them?"

"Oh, that was a glorious day, indeed. Once again she wiped away her tears, but this time they were tears of joy. You see, because she had taken such good care of those plants before the chipmunks showed up, their root system was very strong."

"Is that why you take such good care of me and teach me right from wrong?"

"Yes. If you learn all you can, and try real hard to be the best you can be, then if something happens that sets you back, you don't give up. You have a strong foundation, and with the help of those around you, you can SNAP BACK even better than before."

"Gee, Mom. I thought life was supposed to be easy."

"Life is good, but it's not always easy."

"I'd better put this dirt back before Beulah sees the mess I made."

"Good thinking. Say, when you're done, let's see if we can find some chipmunks to chase."

About the Author

Melinda Spiker Chambers grew up in the rural mountains of central West Virginia in Lewis County. Receiving her BS from West Virginia University and MS from Ohio State University, she is currently a family and consumer science teacher in Romney, WV. She also writes an award-winning column, *Homespun*, for the *Hampshire Review*, and is active with both her church and community. Melinda is also the author of *We Are Whoo We Are* and *Fraidy Cat* and she is a Mom's Choice Award Gold and Silver Honoree for Best Children's Books, Values and Life Lessons. Her **Lessons from Nature Series** has also been named Award Winning Finalist for Best Children's Book Series by the USA

News Best Book Awards. *Fraidy Cat* was also named Finalist for Best Educational Children's Picture Book and Best in Mind/Body/Spirit. Melinda is married to Byron K. Chambers, a retired law enforcement captain with the WV Division of Natural Resources. Together they have two children, Kelly and Chris, and several grandchildren. Raised to have an appreciation for natural beauty, Melinda enjoys looking for the lessons that nature so abundantly teaches to those who take the time to listen.

About the Illustrator

Sue Ann Maxwell Spiker, pictured with her horse, Stonewall, is known for her ability to capture nature's beauty through her watercolor paintings. A native West Virginian, Sue Ann was raised on a farm in Doddridge County where she learned to appreciate the outdoors. Sue Ann often takes her watercolors with her, along with a thermos of coffee, to observe and paint the beautiful scenes of nature. Sue Ann lives on a farm in Jane Lew with her husband, Dr. John Spiker, who is a veterinarian and purebred livestock auctioneer. Sue Ann graduated from Glenville State College with a BA in art education. She and her husband have four children, Jonelle, John Bob, Byron, and David, and several grandchildren. Besides working on the farm, Sue Ann and her husband are active with their church and also own and operate a Guest House.